WHERE THE SEA
Meets the Sky

Peter Bently   Riko Sekiguchi

Sea otter Sophie was out with her mum,
Snuggled up safely on top of her tum.
She gazed through the haze and said by and by:
"What's at the place where the sea meets the sky?"

"The horizon, you mean,"
came her mother's reply.
"No one can reach it
and no one should try.

You might as well swim to
the sun or the moon.
Now I'll go catch a fish and
be back very soon."

But as the mist cleared, Sophie happened to spy
A lighthouse that stood where the sea met the sky.
"That horizon's not far. I think Mum was wrong!
I can easily swim there. It won't take me long."

She swam to the lighthouse,
but saw with dismay
That the edge of the sea
was still far away.

She said to a sunbathing walrus nearby,
"I'm off to the place where the sea meets the sky!"

"Good luck," yawned the walrus, scratching his nose.
"I'd much rather lie on this rock for a doze."

Sophie swam further and after a while,

She spotted a rather peculiar isle.

"I've found the horizon!" she chuckled with glee.

"That island is right where the sky meets the sea!"

Then the isle
SQUIRTED
water

and **FLAPPED**

a great tail.

"I'm not the horizon,"
it laughed. "I'm a . . .

With a
SPLASH
the great whale disappeared
from view.

"Aha!" Sophie chuckled. "I know what to do.
I'll swim underwater and then I can try
To sneak up on the place where the sea meets the sky."

There were all kinds of creatures under the waves.
What fun! Sophie thought as she
swam through some caves.

She saw thin fish and fat fish and whiskery catfish
And slow fish and fast fish and flip-floppy flatfish.

She laughed at a lobster who nibbled her toes
And played with a starfish who danced on her nose.

But then all the fish disappeared in a fright . . .

. . . when some

GREAT HUNGRY SHARKS

swam into sight!

"Yikes!" Sophie panicked and hastily fled.

"It's not very safe underwater!" she said.

"Oh!" Sophie gasped as she came up for air,
"That pesky horizon's still way over there!"

The evening sun was beginning to set.

It's late, Sophie thought, but I won't give up yet.

Sophie swam on . . .

. . . she swam
slower and slower.

She watched the red sun
sinking lower and lower.

She stopped for a rest.
She remembered her mum.
Then she saw with a gasp just
how far she had come.

She was tired and alone in
the deepening dark.
And what was that **RUMBLING?**

Was it a shark?

Then Sophie saw it.
What could it be?
That great looming shape
where the sky met the sea?

A monster was coming,

MASSIVE and **VAST**.

Sophie thought, Yikes!

I'm too tired to swim fast!

It was almost upon her.

"Help!" Sophie cried.

But suddenly – somebody pulled her aside.
The monster sailed past and Sophie soon saw
Just who had saved her by grabbing her paw.

Sophie said, "How did you know where to come?"
"I just asked a **WHALE** and a **WALRUS**," said Mum.

"They said a brave sea otter came swimming by . . .

. . . on her way
to the place . . .

. . . where the sea
meets the sky."

For Tara – P.B.

For Asayo grandma who told me to do the things I love, live life to the fullest

and to my mum who has been incredibly supportive throughout all of this - R.S.

First published in Great Britain in 2020 by Hodder and Stoughton
Text © Peter Bently, 2020 • Illustrations © Riko Sekiguchi, 2020
The moral rights of the author and illustrator have been asserted.
All rights reserved. A CIP catalogue record of this book
is available from the British Library.
HB ISBN: 978 1 44494 630 7 • PB ISBN: 978 1 44494 631 4
10 9 8 7 6 5 4 3 2 1 • Printed and bound in China.

Hodder Children's Books, an imprint of Hachette Children's Group. Part of Hodder and Stoughton
Carmelite House, 50 Victoria Embankment, London EC4Y 0DZ

An Hachette UK Company
www.hachette.co.uk • www.hachettechildrens.co.uk

Hodder
Children's
Books